PUFFIN BOOKS

UK | USA | Australia | Canada | India | Ireland | New Zealand | South Africa

Puffin Books is part of the Penguin Random House group of companies whose addresses can be found at global.penguinrandomhouse.com.

**www.penguin.co.uk**     **www.puffin.co.uk**     **www.ladybird.co.uk**

First published 2017

001

Copyright © Eric Carle LLC, 2017

The moral right of Eric Carle has been asserted

Printed and bound in China

A CIP catalogue record for this book is available from the British Library

ISBN: 978–0–141–37437–6

Eric Carle's name and his signature logotype are trademarks of Eric Carle
To find out more about Eric Carle and his books, please visit **eric-carle.com**
To learn about The Eric Carle Museum of Picture Book Art, please visit
**carlemuseum.org**

All correspondence to: Puffin Books, Penguin Random House Children's
80 Strand, London WC2R 0RL

# I ❤ DAD

with The Very Hungry Caterpillar

## Eric Carle

PUFFIN

# Dad...

# you are easy to

## talk to . . .

## and you're fun to
## play with.

# You can be

# silly...

# but you're still

## cool.

# Even when . . .

# I am feeling
# prickly.

**and I bug you,**

you are

**always**

there . . .

to **catch**

me when I fall.

# That's why...

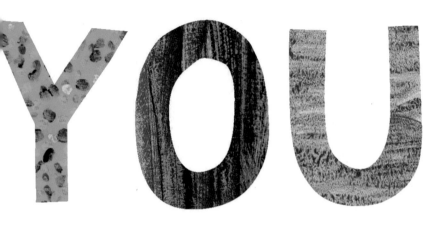

YOU

AD